WHEN YOU NEED A

FRIEND

For Rea (and her new home) x
- S C

For my family and good friends . . .
- C P

First published in Great Britain in 2015 by Little Tiger Press Ltd as *Badger and the Great Storm*

No part of this publication may be reproduced, stored in a retrieval system, or transmitted in any form
or by any means, electronic, mechanical, photocopying, recording, or otherwise, without written
permission of the publisher. For information regarding permission, write to
Little Tiger Press Ltd, 1 The Coda Centre, 189 Munster Road, London, England SW6 6AW.

ISBN 978-0-545-84891-6

12 11 10 9 8 7 6 5 4 3 2   15 16 17 18 19 20/0

Printed in the U.S.A.   40

First Scholastic printing, February 2015

WHEN YOU NEED A FRIEND

Hedgehog's Lettuce Patch

Previously published as *Badger and the Great Storm*

Suzanne Chiew • Caroline Pedler

SCHOLASTIC INC.

"*Mighty oaks from acorns grow!*" sang Badger as he bustled round his cozy burrow. Tucked beneath the roots of the old oak tree, it had always been a happy home for badgers.

Suddenly, there was a squeak at the window.

"Badger!" cried Mouse. "Have you heard? A terrible storm is coming!"

"A storm?" cried Rabbit, hopping up.
"My nest will blow away!" flapped Bird.
"And what about my lettuce garden?"
Hedgehog gasped. "Badger! What should
we do?"

"Don't worry!" smiled Badger. "We'll
make your homes as strong as castles!"

First, Badger made a sturdy door for Rabbit's burrow. "To keep out the wild winds!" he said.

Then, he used some upturned flowerpots to cover Hedgehog's prize lettuces . . .

and built a box around
the nest to keep Bird
safe and dry.

"There!" sighed Badger happily, tying Mouse's ladder in place.

"Thank you, Badger!" Mouse squeaked. "Now please hurry home – the storm is almost here!"

Badger trudged back towards his old oak tree but very soon the rain was pouring down.

"Oh dear!" Badger frowned, as thunder crashed and the wind howled. "Oh dear, oh dear!"

Suddenly a door flew open.
"Badger!" yelled Rabbit. "You
must come in from the storm!"
"It is a bit blustery!" chuckled
Badger, following Rabbit inside.

The baby bunnies gathered round. "Will we get blown away?" they cried. "We're quite safe here," said Badger gently. "Now, who would like a story?" And as they snuggled close, the bunnies soon forgot to be scared.

All through the night, the storm roared and raged. Thunder boomed, lightning flashed and the animals shivered in their homes, waiting for morning to arrive.

But when the sun came up,
the friends had a terrible shock.
  "Where will poor Badger live now?"
gasped Hedgehog. "There have always
been badgers under that old oak tree!"

"He can stay with me," trilled Bird, "though my nest is very high."

"Or with me," suggested Mouse, "though it might be a squeeze."

"He can share with me!" cried Hedgehog. "But we'll need a lot more leaves to snuggle beneath!"

Badger took a deep breath. "Don't worry," he said slowly. "Every problem has a solution!"

When Badger and Rabbit arrived the friends rushed over.
"My poor, poor house," Badger sighed sadly.
"How can we help?" squeaked Mouse.
"Yes, what can we do?" asked Hedgehog.

"First let's rescue my books and gather my pans," called Badger. "Then we'll turn this grand old oak into a brand new house!"

The friends set to work at once. There was a job for everyone, no matter how small.

For days and days
they chopped and
sawed . . .

and hammered and
painted . . .

until they had used
every last piece of
wood to build
something very
special . . .

"My wonderful new home!" beamed
Badger. "You're the best friends I could
ever wish for!"
Just then, Hedgehog rushed over.
"We forgot to use this!" he cried,
holding up a tiny acorn.

"I know just what we'll do with that," said Badger. "Mighty oaks from acorns grow!"

He dug a little hole and they planted it very carefully.

And from that day on, and for ever more, there were always badgers living under the new oak tree.